GRAY FOX

Kenneth R Leonard, Sr

Gray Fox

Copyright @ 2020

by Kenneth R. Leonard, Sr.

Disclaimer

This story is centered around life in the 1800's. The language used in this book reflects the language used during that time period. Some words may be offensive in today's society.

Books by Kenneth R. Leonard, Sr.

The Bible in Poetry for Those Who Do Not
Have Time to Read the Bible, Volumes 1, 2, and 3
Seth Bromley: Circuit Rider
Christmas Memories in Stories & Poems
Cowboy Campfire Poems
Whistle Pig in the Pines
Fool's Gold
Missy
A Bullet for My Brother
Dabsy on Society
Crime Stories: An Anthology
Sol Dorado
Stagecoach West
Skeeter
Stories for the Young at Heart
Spies
Gray Fox

The Texas Slim Series:
Texas Slim: The Beginning
Texas Slim: Sunny
Texas Slim: Ambush Canyon
Texas Slim Under the Texas Sun

Table of Contents

Acknowledgements

Thank you to my sisters, Audrey Smitley, Ethelynn Clark, Diana Wingrove, and Margie Brooks.

A special thank you to my Writer's group: Phyllis Newman, Leslie Robinson, Elizabeth Simmons and Bob Garrett. whose help was greatly appreciated.

God bless you all.

Published by: Kenneth R Leonard, Sr. Publishing Company
1808 Newfield Road Columbus, Ohio 43209

Dedicated to my Children, Grand Children and Great Grand Children. God bless you all.

CHAPTER ONE
Kidnapped

The lazy summer day was waning as the children played in the midst of the water. Gray Fox was a good swimmer for being only five summers old. He could swim under water and enjoyed surprising the others by bobbing up beside them. Their joyful laughter and squeals of delight brought smiles to their mothers, while they scraped hides and did chores in the small Indian camp.

The peaceful village lay on the banks of the big river that flowed south toward the Mexicans. Gray Fox had never been very far away from the village. It was the custom in his village for his Uncle/Father, Standing Elk, to take him fishing in the canoe and hunting in the nearby forest for deer, rabbits and other animals needed for food.

Being so young, Gray Fox was not yet ready for the killing bow, but he had learned tracking and carried the small bow to build his strength.

That evening the Elders talked of the White Eyes. Gray Fox had never seen the White Eyes although he heard them mentioned often during the talks around the fire in the evenings as he leaned against his father's side. The men seemed to hate the White Eyes as their voices rose in discussion.

"They come to take our land," White Feather said. Firelight flickered on his white hair and wrinkled face showing the years he had led his people. Gray Fox watched the Chief's expression harden and his motions grow swift as he talked. "They kill many brother animals and cut down the trees to build tepees that do not move. They have many horses and large animals that have horns." He put his hands to his head with two fingers raised to indicate their horns.

"They need much land for their animals, so cut down many trees so the game moves further away. We now must go many days to find meat to feed our families. This is not good."

"But what can we do?" Standing Elk asked. "They are many and have Thundersticks that kill further than bows can shoot."

"They come like Brother Ant when food is discovered. Everywhere we ride they are there," White Feather said. "We do not trouble the White Eyes for they are too strong for us, but our Enemies do. Although this has been our home and the home of our fathers before us, I think it is time to move closer to Brother Sun when he sleeps." He motioned toward the west.

"But our Enemies live there. How will we survive if we are now in their lands?' Standing Elk cried.

Two Bears laughed. "One of our warriors can kill ten of them. It will not take us long to make a place."

The others nodded and grunted in agreement.

"But we are River People," Lame Dog said. "There is no large water in their land."

White Feather shook his head. "We will send a delegate to ask permission to cross their lands. We do not want our Enemies' land. When I was small, like Gray Fox," he nodded towards Gray Fox, "I heard the Elders speak of a mighty river that lives many moons away. He is called the *Father of Waters*. We will go to that river and make our home."

"This is good," Two Bears said. "You are a wise Chief. Who will you send to talk to our Enemies?"

"You will go. You are well known to our Enemies as a strong warrior. You will take presents for their Chief to indicate we will go through their lands in peace. They may be glad we will no longer be raiding their horses nor killing their warriors." This made the others laugh.

"I will go, my Chief. I will take Gray Fox with me. They will know that I come in peace with my little one at my side."

White Feather nodded. "It is good. They will know we do not want war. You go in two moons."

Gray Fox didn't understand all that was said, but he did get the indication that he was soon to go on a trip. He grew very excited and couldn't wait till the others had left the fire so he could ask his Father.

"Are we leaving, Father?" Gray Fox gazed up into the eyes of his father. Several eagle feathers tied in his long black hair highlighted his athletic build. He was a handsome Indian with high cheeks bones and flashing eyes.

"Yes, we will go to our Enemies to seek permission to travel through their lands to seek a new home."

Gray Fox crossed his arms and stood rigid. "But I like it here, Father. I do not want to leave."

"Neither do we, my Son, but the White Eyes grow strong and will come and take our land and kill our people. We will not be able to stop them because we are few, so it is better for us to go someplace else."

"Won't the White Eyes follow us, Father?"

"Yes, I believe they will, but it will be many moons. You will be a Warrior and have sons of your own by the time they come. So, it is good for us to leave the greedy White Eyes. "

Gray Fox seemed to be thinking. "They must not know the Great Spirit, Father."

"Not all that know the Great Spirit follow his path. But let us talk no more tonight. You need sleep and I must get ready for our journey." He smiled at Morning Dove as they entered the tepee.

"Tomorrow we will get meat so your Mother will have food while we are gone."

Morning Dove was of medium height and her features made her a prize for any Brave, but she only had eyes for Two Bears. "You are leaving, my Husband?"

"Yes. Gray Fox and I will travel to the Enemy camp to seek permission to cross their land and seek a new home near the Father of Waters, where Brother Sun sleeps."

Her brows arched at the news, but she kept her peace.

"The White Eyes are too strong for our small tribe. We will move before we are killed."

CHAPTER TWO

The Raid

Gunfire broke the silence the next morning. Two Bears grabbed his bow and arrows and rushed through the tepee opening. The White Eyes came charging into the camp, guns blazing and yelling. They shot down any Indian they saw. Two Bears was able to shoot several White Eyes before he fell wounded. Gray Fox ran to help his father but was suddenly in the air. He had been swooped up from behind and placed in front of the smelly White Eyes. Screaming and pounding the White Eyes' grizzly face only brought laughter.

"No! No! No! Do not take my son," Morning Dove cried, but was clubbed down amid a menacing laugh.

As fast as the raid had begun it was over. The Raiders had left devastation and death in their wake. Some women, children and a few warriors were left. Tepees were ablaze. Being made of cured animal skins, they burnt quickly.

* * *

As the sun rose on the scene, many women were singing the death song for their husbands, children and loved ones. Morning Dove opened her eyes and tried to stand. Dizziness overcame her and she sank to the ground. Moving her hand to her head she felt blood matting her hair. Using her sleeve, she wiped the blood from her eyes and blinked several times to focus. She fought the sickness and was able to sit and survey the scene. While holding her hand to the back of her head, she found what she had been searching for, the body of Two Bears. Crawling forward, she fought nausea, and was able to reach her fallen husband.

She noticed the gunshot in his shoulder and laid her head on his chest. A faint heartbeat bought gladness to her eyes. She sat beside him and took a deep breath, while thanking the Great Spirit for his life. "His Spirit Guide must be strong to keep him alive," she muttered.

Her head cleared enough to lift Two Bears' shoulder to run her hand underneath to feel where the bullet had exited and smiled. "Good. The bullet has left his body." The hole in the front was bigger than her thumb and the one in the back was larger.

Pushing to her feet, she staggered towards her tepee. It had been spared from the fires that were now smoldering. She fell through the entrance and crawled to where her medicine bag was stored. As she took several deep breaths for strength, she snatched the water bag and put its strap over her shoulder.

She was out of breath when she made it to Two Bears. Washing the wound with water, she made a paste of herbs in a bowl. She sang the healing chant as she worked. Moving closer to Two Bears, she lifted his shoulder and slide her knee underneath to prop him up. Splashing water on the rear wound, she cleaned away the grass and blood and made more herb paste to fill the gaping hole. "Truly Great Spirit, you would not let him live this long and then take his life," she whispered. Finishing the chant, she turned to survey the remains of the camp. She cringed when she saw White Feather crumpled in front of what had been his tepee. The burnt body of Little Flower, his wife, lay across him where she had struggled to reach him with her dying breath. Lying just to the side of them lay his daughter, Snowbird, her husband and their two young children.

Morning Dove closed her eyes to the devastation. They would need a new Chief, she thought. Someone brave and strong that could make decisions for the tribe and lead them to safety. Surveying the camp, she saw only young boys and old ones. Noticing a boy of about ten singing the death chant for his family, she waited till he had finished then called to him. "Running Horse! Come here!"

The boy glanced up and seemed surprised to hear someone call his name.

"Running Horse! Over here!" she motioned with her hand only to bring the dizziness again.

"What is it that you want?" he called. The sadness in the boy's voice made her focus.

"I need to get Two Bears into the tepee. Please help me."

The boy pointed with his hand. "I must bury my family."

"They are dead, Running Horse. You cannot help them. Two Bears still breathes. I need to get him out of Brother Sun."

The boy hesitated. "My family!"

"I will help you with your family, after you help me drag Two Bears into the tepee. I am wounded and cannot do it by myself. We must be careful and not scrape the herbs from the wounds. I will take the wounded arm and you take the other one!"

The boy grew pale as he stared down at the wound and looked as if he were going to throw up.

"Be strong, Running Horse. You are almost at the time to take your warrior trials. This is the beginning of them. It is a different kind of test, but more important than the trials themselves. It is how you conduct yourself now that will determine what kind of warrior you will be. Look around! We have few warriors! You must step forward and become a warrior before your time. There will be no other tests."

Her words seemed to affect the young lad. He straightened his shoulders and puffed out his chest. He supported Two Bears enough so that she could stand. Fighting waves of sickness, she took Two Bears carefully by the shoulder and the rope holding his breechcloth, the cloth that ran between the legs and draped over the rope around his waist in front and back, and dragged him into the tepee.

Propping Two Bears on his right side, she bathed his face to cool his brow. It would be a long night fighting for Two Bears life. Many months of healing would follow.

"I will come help you with your family now. Two Bears will need much rest." She placed her hand on the boy's shoulder. "You have done well. You make your family proud."

Running Horse face beamed with pride.

"You have no family. Would you be kind enough to live with me and help protect Two Bears and me?"

"I will be your protector and provider. I did not see Gray Fox's…" He hesitated in saying the word body.

"He is not here. The White Eyes captured him. I do not know if they kept him or killed him. I cannot go look for him for I must tend to Two Bears. When he is well, he will find his son."

CHAPTER THREE

Cecelia

James Griffin was a man in his late forties. His black hair was gray at the sides with streaks of gray on top. He was over six feet tall with broad shoulders and a slim waist. Leading the raid against the Indian village, he had intended to kill them all and burn their tepees. The murdering Savages had raided his ranch and stolen many of his horses.

They didn't find his horses in the raid, but that didn't matter. They had massacred enough of the tribe that they wouldn't be raiding any more. As he was riding through the camp, killing and burning, he was amazed to see the little boy run out to help his wounded father. The boy's courage made him think of his own son, David, who had died of the grippe, just a few short years ago. He believed Davey would have done the same thing and without thinking he had caught the boy up and placed him in front of him on the saddle.

He missed his own son. He would raise the boy as his own. True, he couldn't replace Davey, but it might help to fill the hollow spot he felt in his chest since

Davey died. He longed to see the little fellow running around and imitating him again. It had always brought a smile to his face and a hearty laugh from his belly.

His big arm encircled the little body to keep him from fighting. This little one had spunk, just like Davey. Davey's clothes were still in the trunk. If he cut the boy's hair and put human clothes on him, in a few years people may not even know he was an Indian. The sun out here burnt many a man darker than this boy's skin.

A thought marred James's thinking. How would Cecelia take to the boy?" He knew she missed Davey and still mourned for him, so maybe she would welcome the little tyke. Would luck be on his side?

He had to keep one hand on the boy as he dismounted. The little fellow didn't know the way, but he was determined to go home. James laughed and catching the boy by the back of his breechcloth string, he carried him into the house.

Cecelia glanced up from her rocker as horror crossed her face. Her white hair protruded from beneath her dust cap. It gave her dark eyes a glaring effect. Her pug nose and small mouth hid the venom that spilled forth.

"James, why on earth are you dragging that heathen child into my Christian home?"

James grinned. "He's an orphan, so I thought we could raise him till he's big enough to shoot."

"Well, take him out of here and throw him into the hog pen. They'll get rid of him quick enough."

"Aw now, you don't mean that. Why, he's not big enough to hurt a fly. Wouldn't you like to have someone around to fetch firewood and such?"

"Are you daffy? He couldn't carry more than one puny little stick at a time. By the time he got enough wood the fire would be out. Put him out in the barn and then get rid of him tomorrow. I don't want him around. I can smell him from over here. It isn't Christian to have a Heathen in the house."

"Well, he's young enough you could make him a Christian. Ain't that what we're supposed to be doing, anyway? Converting them!"

"They have to have a brain first, so they can understand. He doesn't look smart enough to feed himself."

"Aw, come on. Give him a chance. He ain't much different then those Slaves your Grandpa had before he gambled the plantation away."

Anger flashed in Cecelia's dark eyes. "How many times do I have to tell you that the gambling man cheated Gramps? That's why he shot him. He tried to explain it to the Judge, but he wouldn't listen and hung Gramps any ways. Then he made us move for spite."

"Well, I was sorry your Grandpa got hung, but if you still lived on that plantation, I would never have got to marry you. As it was, none of them rich boys wanted to marry you after your Grandpa was hung for murder."

"I don't want to talk about it, and I'll thank you not to bring it up anymore. At least the Slaves could talk so you could understand them, although I never associated with them, other than to tell them what to do." She nodded at Gray Fox. "I can't understand a word of his gibberish."

"Aw, He's got spunk. You should've seen him trying to help his father after I shot him with my buffler gun. Blew a hole in him bigger than a saucer."

"If you going to keep him, you'll have to sleep in the barn with him."

James jerked his head up as fear etched his face. "You don't mean that Cecelia, Darling."

"Well, how are you going keep him from running away?"

James rubbed his whiskers and then snapped his fingers. "I'll put him in the root cellar and put that trunk over the lid. That'll keep him."

That night, James held Gray Fox's arms and lowered him into the dark hole. He dropped the lid and stomped it in place. He slid the trunk over it and sat on it. "There now. Snug as a bug. You can hardly hear him screaming. When we get into bed, we won't be able to hear him at all."

"You better find something to do with him. You can't keep him down there forever. I have to get my food out."

"Maybe he'll grow on you, once we cut his hair and put some clothes on him."

"Where are you going to get clothes…?" Her eyebrows shot up and her mouth dropped. "Not Davey's clothes!"

"They're just lying there rotting away. The Doctor said we can't have any more kids, so what're we going to do with them?"

"I'm not putting Little Davey's clothes on any Savage!"

"Cecelia, you can change him and teach him Christian ways. I know you can."

"I'm going to bed. You're supper's in the warmer."

"Ain't you even gonna dish it up for me?"

"No. I'm not rewarding you for bringing that Heathen Brat into my home. You can get your own breakfast, too."

"Aw Cecelia. Don't be like that."

She gave James a look that made his heart stop. He watched till she slammed the bedroom door.

James shook his head. "That's what you get when you try to do a Christian deed. I thought sure she would like the little fellow. He stood and patted the trunk. "I'll see you in the morning. Maybe she'll feel better about letting you stay."

It was all James could do to cut Gray Fox's hair the next day and put clothes on him. Fighting, clawing, scratching and biting, not to mention the stream of words that Gray Fox uttered helped the matter any.

Tears streamed down Cecelia's face when she saw Gray Fox in Davy's outfit. "I'll never forgive you for putting those clothes on him," she said and stormed into the bedroom, slamming the door for punctuation.

James looked down into Gray Fox's upturned face. "I think you look great, Cowboy. You're just a little shaver. I think I'll call you Pee Wee. How do you like that name?"

Gray Fox didn't smile and tried to pull the shirt off, but the suspenders kept it in place.

"I thought you'd like that name. Kind of fits you. Here, let's have some breakfast. You want some jelly bread?"

Gray Fox stared at the out-stretched hand. James smiled and took a big bite of bread and then offered it again. Gray Fox bent over and bit apiece off and his eyes lit up at the sweet taste. He took the bread and shoved it all in his mouth. It made his mouth too full to chew properly. James broke out laughing.

"I thought you'd like that. Cecelia makes the best biscuits I've ever ate. Here, try some of these eggs. See, you can dip the bread into the yolk and it's good." James dipped and ate, then offered Gray Fox a bite. Gray Fox almost bit his finger in his eagerness to eat. He smacked Gray Fox across the face so hard, the boy staggered back. "Hey, careful now. I need them fingers to feed myself. You got to learn to eat right."

James finished his breakfast without a glance at the tears slipping down Gray Fox's face. He didn't offer him any more food. "Come on, we got chores to do. Stop that sniffling!" Another crack on the cheek stopped Gray Fox's tears. "You got to wear them shoes. Those flimsy things you had, I burnt with the rag you were wearing. They wouldn't last no time doing ranch chores." Thinking of Cecelia's reaction his feelings for the boy quickly waned.

James gave Gray Fox a jerk and he almost flew after him. James pointed to the bucket on the porch. "That there is slop for the hogs. Pick it up and take it to the hog pen."

When Gray Fox didn't move, James jerked him by the arm and forced his hand around the handle. "Pick it up and carry it, you Heathen. Can't you learn anything?"

Gray Fox had to use two hands to carry the bucket. The smell from the sty almost made him sick. When he saw the pigs grunting and clamoring for the trough, he dropped the bucket and ran away.

"Gall darn you, come back here. This here is going to be one of your chores. You almost spilt the slop."

Another crack set Gray Fox's ears ringing. "Now when I tell you to do something, you do it. Hear!"

Dragging Gray Fox by the arm, James grabbed the bucket and headed to the hog pen. Placing Gray Fox on a stump he gave him the bucket. "Now, dump it in the trough before I throw you in there with 'em. You're gonna be more trouble than you're worth." Fear rode Gray Fox's eyes as he dumped the bucket.

"Hey, careful there. You're dumping it on the hogs. They can't eat if off their heads. Durn stupid Heathen."

The morning passed slowly as James tried to teach Gray Fox chores. His hand got tired of hitting the boy and yelling at him to pay attention. He was glad when Cecelia rang the dinner bell.

She stood at the door with her arms crossed. "He can eat on the porch." She pointed to a tin plate sitting on the corner. Birds were flapping and pecking at it and a string of ants were crawling all over it.

James tied a rope around a post and around Gray Fox's neck. He pointed to the plate and commanded. "Eat!" He entered the house.

Gray Fox sat beside the plate and brushed the ants off the jelly bread. He woofed it down and then stared at the beans. He touched them and licked his fingers. He picked up a bean, brushed the ant off and popped it in his mouth. It was a new taste but one that wasn't so bad. He was licking the plate when James came out the door.

A swat on the side of the head made Gray Fox drop the plate. "You got to wash that clean not lick it. Oh well, it's your plate. I guess you can clean it anyway you want."

CHAPTER FOUR
Running Horse

Running Horse crouched in the bushes and watched James teaching Gray Fox. He barely recognized him in those White Boy's clothes and short hair. But it had to be Gray Fox the way he was being treated. The women in camp beat prisoners into submission and maybe that was what was happening to Gray Fox.

Running Horse wished there was a way he could free his little friend, but the White Eyes never left Gray Fox alone. Running Horse could hear the smacks Gray Fox received and hate burned in his eyes. He thought of shooting the White Eyes with an arrow, but the distance was too far. If he had a horse and knew how to ride, he could charge in and shoot the White Eyes before he had time to react. The sun burning the side of his face reminded Running Horse it was time to go. He was supposed to be out hunting and not watching Gray Fox.

It had been easy to follow the trail. Running Horse could follow little animals like rabbits, squirrels and raccoon. The White Eyes left so big a trail Running Horse didn't even have to stop and check it. The ground was tore up from the metal the White Eyes put on their ponies feet.

Running Horse watched Gray Fox and wished he could signal him that he was here. As he moved to a better position, his eye caught the movement in the corral. There were a few horses grazing there. One looked a little better than the others. They would need a horse to pull Two Bears on a travois. Reluctantly, he moved away from the safety of the bush and crawled to the corral. He found a lead rope hanging on a post.

The horses began to mill around and snort at the strange smell. Running Horse slipped into the corral and raced to the horse. He grabbed it around the neck before it could run. The horse threw his head and reared trying to get the creature off, but Running Horse hung on. He hooked the lead rope to the hackamore, or bitless bridal, and talking softly he led the horse to the gate. He had just cleared the gate when the boom of the rifle sounded and scared him. The bullet hit the post where his head had been just a second before.

"Thieving Redskin! Steal a man blind!" James yelled reloading his rifle.

Running Horse didn't bother to close the gate and that's what saved his life. The White Eyes was running towards the corral to save his horses that were following Running Horse through the gate. Running Horse led the horse at a fast trot till he came to a stump. He stood on the stump and laid straight across the horse's back.

Fear made the horse break into a run, bouncing Running Horse up and down as he hung onto the mane and lead rope.

Running Horse stayed on till the horse slowed and stopped for breath. He slid from its back and wondered why anyone would want to ride such a bumpy animal. He was shaken so badly he had to lean against the horse to clear his head. The smell of the horse sweat made him think of his father, Standing Elk.

Standing Elk, often smelled of horse for he was an excellent horse rider and trainer. "I will be like my father and train this horse to let me ride. After I learn to ride, I can come back and rescue Gray Fox." Leading the horse, he headed home. He was able to gradually make friends by feeding the horse bits of grass. He knew the correct position to ride was sitting up, so he used a big rock to climb onto the horse. Urging it into motion, he found this way of riding much more comfortable than riding on his stomach.

Running Horse was now able to see further ahead and was happy to see deer feeding in a meadow. He guided the horse into a group of oak trees and tied it to a sapling. Slowly making his way to the edge of the trees, he made sure he had the wind against him to hide his smell. Waiting till the deer moved closer in their feeding, he rose up and shot a large buck. It startled the others into flight as it ran a few feet before it collapsed.

Running Horse yelled his victory cry as he bounded across the field to the deer. He checked to make sure it was dead and withdrew his arrow. The problem now was how to get the deer onto the horse's back? Taking one end of the lead rope he tied it around the deer's neck. While making the horse back up, he lifted the deer's head so the antlers would not dig into the ground and let the carcass slide on the grass. He stopped at a large rock and used it to place the deer across the horse's back. This took a while, as the horse was not happy with the smell of the dead animal. He strung the rope under the horse's belly and tied the deer to its back. Stepping on the rock, he sprang behind the deer and headed to the village.

* * *

The little band was forming up to move as Running Horse came into camp the next day. A broad smile crossed Morning Dove's face as she watched Running Horse approach.

"You make a fine provider Running Horse. I see you have found a friend to help you in hunting." She moved to help unload the deer. "We will be able to share some of the meat with the others that have no provider."

A large grin broke across his face. "I have good news. Gray Fox is alive."

Morning Dove froze as she heard the news. "Where is he? Is he well?"

"He is at the place of the White Eyes. They have cut his hair and put their clothes on him. He is not happy. They hit him often to make him learn their ways."

Morning Dove sagged against the horse as her heart leaped. Her little boy was among the cruel White Eyes. How could she endure when she knew he was suffering? It was impossible to go to him and leave Two Bears for there was no one to tend his wounds and care for him. Surely, he would die if she left him.

Agony etched her face as she helped Running Horse hang the deer. Her expert skinning had the hide off and the deer portioned while Running Horse watered the horse. "Take portions to the different families that need meat." He didn't have time to take bows for the little procession was already on the trail.

* * *

Morning Dove made a travois by tying skins across two lodge poles. They drug Two Bears onto it. The new deer hide was folded and placed at the foot of the travois to be scraped and dried at a later time. Running Horse was glad the Great Spirit had provided the horse for he did not think Morning Dove would have the strength to drag her husband's travois, even though her head wound was a little better.

Morning Dove softly sang a chant to the Great Spirit to protect her son as each step took her further away. The knowledge that he was alive was little comfort knowing how he was treated. Her laughing son was the joy and breath in her life and to lose him, even for a little while, was heart breaking.

* * *

They made the Enemy camp in two days and were met by a delegation. "You are not welcome," Chief Running Dog said.

"It is you raiding the White Eyes that caused us to lose our homes," Morning Dove explained.

"What is that to us. The White Eyes steal our land and kill our animals. It is right to raid them. Your Braves are weak like Squaws not to raid them."

"You know our Braves were strong Warriors," Morning Dove said. "You have fought them many times and lost. Our great Chief, White Feather, said the White Eyes Thundersticks make them too strong for us. He was going to send Two Bears, my husband, to ask you to let us cross your land, so that we may go to the Father of Waters to make a new home. In return, you could have our land."

Running Dog seemed please at the prospect of gaining their land.

After much discussion, it was decided they could camp in the far section till their wounds healed and made travel easier. "We will not provide food, shelter, protection, or supply any of your needs. The White Eyes do not worry us. We are strong and soon we will have

Thundersticks to defeat them. They are a good source of raids for horses and helping the young Braves to become Warriors. Since there are so many White Eyes, we raid them often. Go!" He pointed west to the edge of their land.

Morning Dove soon had the tepee erected and Two Bears comfortable. The meat was roasted over an open fire and she mashed small portions and made a broth for Two Bears.

"I will keep my horse staked by the tepee," Running Horse said. "I have seen some of their boys and young men eyeing it. I will nap during the day and keep watch at night. With the help of the Great Spirit we will soon leave this place."

CHAPTER FIVE

Pee Wee

On the third day after his arrival, he screamed and fought when James tried to put him in the dark and musty root cellar. "All right, Pee Wee, but if you try to escape, I'll hog tie you and throw you down there every night for as long as you live."

James tied the rope around Pee Wee's neck and the other end to the leg of the heavy oak table. "I don't think you'll be able to lift that leg till you're a mite older. I built it pretty solid."

Pee Wee didn't try to escape. He had nowhere to go. Being only five years old he wouldn't be able to survive the trek to find a friendly tribe or a place to live. He would have to wait till he was older and stronger. Lying on the floor reminded him of the hard ground of the tepee. The heat from the coals in the fireplace kept him warm and reminded him of the many times he had sat with his father and the men as they talked, discussed problems, told stories and jokes at the campfire. He had seen his parents go down at the hand of James and that was something he wasn't able to forget or forgive.

James turned to Cecelia. "I can't see why you can't make up with the boy. You treat him like a dog."

Anger flashed across her face. "He's disgracing my Davey's clothes."

Following her into the bedroom he said, "He would gladly shed them if I'd let him, but he needs something to wear while doing chores. You don't want him running around nakked."

* * *

Through James' method of teaching, Gray Fox soon knew to answer to Pee Wee and to learn the English language. He had seen Running Horse take the horse and tried to run to him, but James had grabbed him. Later, Pee Wee decided it couldn't have been him. He was too young to be out raiding and stealing horses. He didn't think his parents were alive, so believed that the tribe had perished. Though the thief looked to be from his tribe, he would not have recognized Gray Fox in the White Eyes clothes, so there was no chance of rescue. If there were any of the tribe left, they were going to move further towards Father Sun, so they would not be concerned with the struggles of a small orphan boy. He settled to his fate to survive.

The clothes were too confining and heavy in the summertime. Pee Wee longed for the time he could shed his shirt and feel Brother Sun on his skin.

James didn't bother to teach him the skills he needed to survive in the woods. He was more concerned with his learning women's work of feeding the animals and cleaning stalls. Pee Wee wasn't able to carry full buckets of water, so he had to make twice as many trips, which didn't please James at all. He seemed to fail to realize Davey had been older than Pee Wee.

"I don't know why you're so weak. Davey could tote a full bucket. I guess you Savages ain't as strong as us White Folk. Can't you work faster, it takes forever for you to muck out a stall."

It took a while for Pee Wee to understand that James was not talking to him, but down to him. The tone of his voice told Pee Wee that James was not praising him.

* * *

After six months, James no longer tied Pee Wee to the table leg. When he was left untied doing chores, Pee Wee made no effort to try and escape. The drudgery of the ranch life wore on. Pee Wee couldn't understand why the White Eyes kept so many animals when they didn't do anything with them but watch them eat. They cut the grass, stored it and fed it to the animals during the times of cold. One of his chores was to stand in the back of the wagon and throw out the dead grass with a forked tool, but some of the animals still died. "Why don't you just eat buffalo and not have to do all the things to keep the animals alive?" he had asked.

James had cuffed him on the head. "Boy, you're some kind of stupid, you know that?"

Pee Wee hated the hogs and the chickens were always under foot causing him to trip and fall. He enjoyed the eggs but hated trying to gather them. "They hurt my hands for taking the eggs."

"That's 'cause they want to set and hatch chicks, but I want them eggs for breakfast."

Never-the-less, every spring a hen would come traipsing in with a bunch of chicks behind her that needed fed and watered. They were cute when small, but their stench as they grew made them unbearable. The male would jump at him and flap its wings causing pain.

"Quick torturing that rooster," James would yell.

Pee Wee keep an eye on the rooster, but sometimes it attacked from ambush. Pee Wee was glad when it got trampled under the wagon. He enjoyed digging the hole and putting what was left in Mother Earth.

* * *

As Pee Wee grew James found clothes for him at the church since he couldn't wear David's anymore. He didn't bother to make them fit, so they hung on Pee Wee's growing body. He was glad that they were not tight, but they got in the way when he was trying to do chores.

Pee Wee would secretly gaze at Brother Sun as it sat on the western horizon and longed for the freedom of the woods. The 50 caliber Sharps rifle that James kept close by was too heavy for Pee Wee to learn to shoot. "Someday I will leave this place and find a good place to live," he whispered.

* * *

One night, Pee Wee was staring out the window, dreaming of being with his people again, when he saw movement down by the corral. Watching carefully, he made sure of what he saw then rapped on James's door. "The Enemy is here."

James came running out in his nightshirt and killed them before they could take the horses. This endeared him to James in that he could warn him when the Enemy was after the horses. James' way of burying them was to tie a rope to their legs and drag them off into the woods for the wolves and birds to devour. Pee Wee didn't care for they were the Enemy, not his tribe.

"You're the best hound I've ever had," James said and rubbed Pee Wee's head. Pee Wee smiled up at him, welcoming the kind words even after he found out what the word hound meant.

"Ain't you ever going to let him eat at the table, Cecelia?"

"I do declare, James, you know it isn't proper. He's a Savage. He doesn't eat proper, licking his fingers and wiping the grease on his arms. He needs to bathe every night to keep the smell down."

Pee Wee didn't mind eating on the porch. It reminded him of eating outside the tepee. The house, as he learned it was called, was too cramped. The White Eyes had too much stuff crammed into every corner and built places to store even more. He longed for the sparseness of the tepee, where they kept only the necessities.

He longed for the freedom of the camp and playing with the other children. Remembering the wrestling matches with Running Horse and the other boys brought a lump to his throat and tears to his eyes. He missed his mother's love, her cooking and the hunting and fishing trips with his uncle/father. He longed for the campfires and the men's hearty laughter when they told jokes or played pranks. He had seen White Feather and his family die. The old Chief had been kind to him and was like his Grandfather. His real Grandfather, Big Bear, had died in battle years ago.

CHAPTER SIX

Round Up

The Ranchers had gathered for Round Up and James hired a few men from town for the roping and branding. Some men were assigned to round up the new calves, rope them and bring them to the fire to be branded.

Pee Wee remembered his first Round up. He hated branding. He disliked the burnt smell as the hot iron was applied to the little calves.

Pee Wee wrinkled his nose. "Why do you burn them?"

"How dumb can you be?" James said. "It don't hurt them. We just burn the hair in the shape of the brand. Brands are needed to tell who the cattle belong to, otherwise, one person could claim them all."

"Why would you want to do that? There are so many."

James shook his head. "The more you have the richer you are. You can sell them for money to buy things."

"These animals are not as good as buffalo. Buffalo feed themselves. We use horses for trade because they are better. We can ride them and trade them for wives. Do you trade cattle for wives?"

"No, we're not Savages. We marry for love," Newt Sweeney, the crusty old man was dressed in dirty buckskins and looked like a mountain man with his grizzly beard and long hair, although he had never been one.

Pee Wee looked confused. "Do you not give their father payment for a Squaw?"

"You ask too many questions," Newt said. "Take this brand and put it in the fire."

"I want to know?" Pee Wee shoved the iron into the fire. He watched Newt notch the calf's ear. "Why do you cut their ears?"

"So, we can tell who they belong," James replied.

"You said the brands do that," Pee Wee nodded towards the calf.

"Brands can be changed, but notched ears can't."

"Then why not just notch the ears?" Pee Wee had asked.

"This is the dumbest Redskin I've ever met," Newt replied after notching an ear. "You can see the notch from afar, but you have to get right up on "em to see the brand."

Pee Wee looked at the brand and the notched ear. He had to be close to see either one. Maybe the White Eyes could see further than he could? "Why do you cut them there?"

"We don't need a lot of bulls," James said. "They will fight and gouge each other with their horns to be boss, so we make steers out of them and they're easier to handle."

Pee Wee had seen the males fight and the results. Sometimes the loser had to be destroyed and eaten. The White Eyes ways were just too confusing. "Why do you cut their tails? They can't kill flies."

"We bob the tails of the ones we are going to sale," James said. "It makes it easy to spot them and cut them out of the herd."

"You're driving me crazy with all your questions," Newt commanded. "Go untie that calf and bring it here to be branded."

Pee Wee went to the tree and untied the calf. It was as big as he was and decided to go back to its Mama, dragging Pee Wee along behind it.

Newt rolled on the ground with laughter as a laughing James shouted. "Stop playing with that calf and bring it here!"

Slipping and sliding, Pee Wee fought the calf for control. As he neared its Mama, the calf's bawling brought her on the run. Pee Wee dropped the rope and ran. The crew slapped their knees and laughed as Pee Wee ran as fast as he could for the tree. He made it to the first limb just as the cow caught up to him.

When the men controlled their laughter, Newt rode over and took Pee Wee from the tree. "Ya dumb Injun," he cried. "Now I have to catch that calf all over again. I ought to spank your tail." He gave Pee Wee several swats on the rump and stood him on the ground.

Pee Wee headed back to the fire.

"Why did you let it go," James scolded. "You can't do anything right. Get some buffler chips out of the wagon so we can keep this branding fire going. If you keep letting them loose, we're going to be here all day."

Later that afternoon, Newt said it would be a grand entertainment to put Pee Wee on the back of a calf and see if he could ride it. The men enjoyed seeing Pee Wee falling off, so kept putting him on different calves. It wasn't long before they chose larger calves and see Pee Wee thrown into the air as the calves twisted and turned to get the strange weight from their backs.

By the time Pee Wee was a few years older, he was put on grown bulls for he had learned to stay aboard for several seconds. Another sport the men enjoyed was to have Pee Wee try to Bulldog calves. Instead of dropping from a horse and grabbing the calves head and twisting it till the calf flopped over, Pee Wee was to lasso it, hand walk the rope, while holding the calf steady, till he got to the head, then try and bulldog the calf. The men howled with laughter as Pee Wee was drug and tossed about.

Eventually, Pee Wee could lasso a calf and bring it to the branding fire. He could lasso, throw the calf and tie its feet in a few seconds. James wouldn't allow him to compete in any of the local rodeos after he won all the events in one. The prizes went to the second-place winner for they couldn't have an Indian beating the White boys in all the events. Pee Wee didn't care. The honor came in winning, not in the prizes.

James still didn't let him ride horses for fear he would escape. Pee Wee could brand, notch ears, castrate and bob tails. He soon knew which calves would be kept and which ones were to be sold. The men still teased him, but not as much.

CHAPTER SEVEN

Town

The glaring sun made the trip to town uncomfortable as Pee Wee rode in back of the bouncing wagon. The land did not look bare to him as he surveyed it to the horizon. To walk or ride over it in freedom was one of his greatest desires. He had made this trip to town every year and was referred to as Breed or Chief, whenever visitors came to the ranch or they went to town. Pee Wee sat on the steps to the General Store.

"I don't want no thieving Savages in here. They'll steal anything that ain't nailed down," Barnaby Stillman had yelled, when Pee Wee first entered the store years ago. "Keep him outside. I got civilized Christian folks in here."

Pee Wee watched the two boys, approach. "Stand up!" You a real Indian?" Bucky Clayburn sneered as Pee Wee stood. "Ya don't look like no Indian."

Pee Wee stared at Bucky, who appeared to be a little older than Pee Wee's ten years.

"What's the matter? Can't you talk?" Wally Bishop asked.

Pee Wee turned to look at Wally who was the same size as him.

"Cat's got his tongue," Bucky said, and the two boys laughed.

"I don't think he's a real Indian. He don't look scary to me," Wally said puffing out his chest.

"You ain't got no War Paint, Tomahawk, or Bow and Arrows," Wally cried. "If you're a real Indian where's all your stuff?"

"Aw, he ain't no Indian," Bucky said and gave Pee Wee a push backward. "Hey, that's my shirt!" Bucky cried. "See, that little tear there where I caught it on a bramble bush. Give me my shirt. You stole it." Bucky began to tear the shirt off Pee Wee.

"Yeah, I remember that. I was with you when you tore it," Wally lied.

Bucky held up the torn shirt. "Ain't no good now. You tore it. I ought to punch you in the nose for stealing my shirt and tearing it up."

Men and women gathered on the porch and were grinning while watching the two boys hurrahing Pee Wee. Wally had slipped down behind Pee Wee and was keeling on his hands and knees. Bucky gave Pee Wee a shove and over he went to the delight of the crowd.

Pee Wee remembered the trick as the start of wrestling in the tribe and sprang to his feet. He dove over Wally and took a surprised Bucky to the ground. Sitting across Bucky's chest he pinned him to the ground.

"Get off of me!" Bucky shouted. He tossed Pee Wee aside as if he were a flower. Scrambling to his feet Bucky braced his legs. "So, you want to fight? Come on."

Pee Wee crawled to his feet. Bucky delivered a right cross that sent him sprawling. The men clapped their hands and slapped their knees enjoying the show.

Pee Wee wiped the blood from his nose, moved to a crouch position and charged. "OOF!" came from a surprised Bucky as Pee Wee's head caught Bucky in the stomach and the two boys went to the ground.

Wally saw his chance and jumped on Pee Wee's back. Rolling on the ground, the two boys struggled for a hold. Having someone his own size made it easier for Pee Wee to wrestle. He had often wrestled Running Horse as part of his training and enjoyed the fun. Running Horse had taken it easy on him, but these boys seemed to be angry.

Wally was able to get free and cracked Pee Wee on the jaw with a short jab. Pain flashed through Pee Wee's brain. This was not what wrestling had been like in the village. Wally struggled to his feet, braced his feet and waited for Pee Wee to stand.

"Come on. You hurt Bucky's stomach and now I'm going to hurt you."

Pee Wee thought of Running Horse's favorite tricks. He dodged Wally's wild swing, wrapped his arms around him and flipped him over his hip. Wally hit the ground with a surprise thud.

Getting to his feet Wally cried, "I'd like to see you try that again." Wally charged and Pee Wee went to the ground with the momentum, caught Wally in the stomach with his feet and flipped him over his head. Seeing Pee Wee getting the better of the two bullies, Newt Sweeny came running and grabbed Pee Wee, shaking him like an old rag. "Here! Here! You're fighting dirty! You can't use them Indian tricks on these boys. Filthy Redskin."

James came to the porch. "What're you doing, Newt?"

"This here red Brat you brought to town with you is fighting dirty."

James gave Pee Wee a cuff on the head. "Can't you even behave yourself like decent folks? I'm sorry, Boys, but I haven't got him trained yet. He don't know how to behave in town. I'll give him a licking soon as we get home."

"Don't wait!" Newt yelled. "It's never too late to learn him how to behave with decent folks. "

James spun Pee Wee and gave him a boot in the rear that liftcd him off the ground.

"Kick him again," Newt cried in glee. "One more won't hurt him and might teach him a lesson."

James booted him again. "Now, get in the wagon and behave yourself. I see I can't bring you to town till I learnt you some proper manners."

Bucky and Wally grinned as they brushed the dust from their clothes.

The wagon jostled and jolted Pee Wee as they headed to the ranch. Confusion reigned as Pee Wee thought about the incident. The boys wanted to wrestle, but then they got angry. White Eyes just don't make any sense, he thought. They want to do something but get angry if it don't come out the way they want. Just like tomorrow, when they will make the trip to the building, they call a Church, but they wouldn't obey what the man says.

* * *

Sitting under the tree he was tied to, Pee Wee was able to hear the man dressed in black talking, so the people inside had to be able to hear him. The man yelled every so often, like James did when he was angry. Maybe that is why the people don't listen to him. Every Sunday he told them about their Great Spirit, but no one did what the man said. They were the same afterwards as they were before. If they weren't going to do what they were told, why did they come?

"Love your neighbor as yourself," the man thundered. Pee Wee overheard conversations and the people didn't even like their neighbors. A lot of them they hated. They sang about love and going to a place called Heaven, but no one did what the man said to get there. It was not like the tribe, where everyone shared and did what was best for all. Here, everyone was the enemy even if they were related.

Pee Wee watched the little white clouds drifting by as if pulled by an invisible string across the blue sky. Was their Great Spirit the same as his Great Spirit? White Eyes believed that people went up there when they died, but he couldn't see anyone. If they went there, why did they put them in the ground inside trees they called coffins and pile Mother Earth on them instead of putting them in a tree or on a platform so their spirits could easily be free?

* * *

Pee Wee looked at his calloused hands. He longed for the feel of a bow and arrow. He could lasso a horse, find a hen hatching her eggs in the brush, and pull a calf from the mud. He had a way with animals but disliked the ranch animal's smell and the constant meaningless chores they caused.

James loved to see Pee Wee tossed high in the air from a bucking bronco. As he grew, James began putting him on the wildest broncs to the men's delight. Pee Wee was thrilled to be on a horse and did his best to stay aboard. This was more like what he wanted to do. The time on the calves and bulls meant for entertainment served Pee Wee well and he quickly became adept to busting broncs. James kept trying to find mean ones to toss him off.

"Concern Indian." James threw his hat on the ground. "You'd think he was born to bust broncs. I can't see how anyone that young can stay aboard."

"Well, I hear there's a black stallion over to Bob Jergens'," Newt said. "He's a mean one that's throwed every top bronc fighter that got on him. But you don't want him, he might kill the boy," Newt said slyly. "But if you've a mind to get him, I reckon Bob might trade him for a few good mares. He's mighty disgusted feeding that black for nothing."

James perked up. "A stallion. New blood. That's what I need to build my herd."

"Bob ain't put him in with no mares," Newt added. "He's afraid he'd kill them."

"A stallion ain't agonna kill any mares", James muttered looking in the direction of Bob's ranch.

"This one might." Newt said. "He tries to kick down the corral when any other horse is near, mare or stallion."

James surveyed his horses. "If he's like you say, Bob might be happy to get rid of him cheap. I could part with that Bay, the Roan and maybe that Brown, if I have to give three. I better ride over there and see what he'd take." James saddled his horse. "Pee Wee!" James called, "Mount up! Going to look at a horse."

"I wouldn't put that boy on that stallion," Newt taunted.

"Pee Wee can ride him," James said mounting and turning his horse towards the lane. Pee Wee followed on an old nag. James knew the horse couldn't run fast so was not afraid of Pee Wee trying to escape.

* * *

Bob Jergens was a tall lanky man. Disgust rode his features as he watched the trio approach. "Why did you have to bring that fool Indian along?"

"He's my broc buster. He can ride anything."

While the men talked, Pee Wee sat on the fence and watched the Black in the corral. It's mean eye and flashing hoofs, as it kicked up its tail, told him it was a bad one. It was pure terror on hoofs.

"I'll bring the horses over for your inspection," James said. "Put a rope on that stallion, Pee Wee."

Pee Wee eased out a loop and opened the gate. He kept an eye on the Black as he closed the gate. When it charged, he moved his horse sideways and dropped the loop over the stallion's head. Pee Wee guided his horse back as the stallion reared and tried to kill the horse with flashing hoofs.

Pee Wee could feel the fear in his horse as he maneuvered it out of harm's way, keeping the rope taunt. Pee Wee's horse stumbled just as the stallion charged and sent horses and rider into the dust. Pee Wee rolled and jumped across his horse. He mounted the stallion as it gained its feet.

Bucking, crow-hopping and sun fishing kept Pee Wee using every ounce of strength to stay aboard. Spinning to the left and then right sent Pee Wee flying. Struggling to his feet he dove to the side as the stallion came rushing.

"What are you doing, Pee Wee?" James called with a wide grin at seeing Pee Wee in distress. "I told you to put a rope on him, not play with him. Now, grab that rope and let's get going."

Pee Wee rolled and caught the rope as it went by. He didn't have time to stand as the stallion began dragging him around the corral. Pee Wee hung onto the rope as he was whirled around and around in the dust to the delight of the men watching.

The stallion tried to dust him off with the tethering pole, but Pee Wee saw it coming and rolled the opposite way, making the rope wind onto the pole as the stallion ran in circles. In a few seconds, the rope was too short for the stallion to move.

Pee Wee talked and soothed the frightened animal. He breathed into its nostrils as he had seen his father do. He ran his hands along the neck and flanks cooing soft words. The wildness left its eyes as it snorted and tossed its head.

"Are you going to take all day," James chided. "We'll miss supper."

Pee Wee continued brushing with his hand and softly talking to the horse. He was finally able to calm it down. Unwinding the rope, he led the horse to the gate.

James ignored the bruises and blood on Pee Wee as he studied the horse Pee Wee had ridden. "Gonna have to shoot that horse. Why on earth did you take it in there?"

Pee Wee looked over his shoulder at the old crippled horse. He felt bad about it having to be destroyed, but knew if he had entered the corral on foot, he would be dead now. The crack of the rifle did nothing to console his misery.

James mounted and headed home without a look back. Bob stood with mouth open as Pee Wee walked behind James leading the stallion.

"I would never have believed it if I hadn't seen it with my own eyes," Newt said.

Bob removed his hat and ran his fingers through his sweaty hair. "I never thought anyone would get that close to that stallion, let alone lead him on a rope."

"That Indian put a spell on that horse," Newt offered.

"He done something to it," Bob said. "He might lead it, but I guarantee you he won't ride it. That horse has tossed some of the best riders I could find. Ain't nobody going to ride him."

Newt turned to look at the dead horse. "I'm hoping that stallion will break that boy's fool neck. Ain't right an Indian living with White Folk. Nothing good will come of it, you wait and see. "Soon as that Breed gets old enough, he's going to murder them in their bed."

CHAPTER EIGHT

Broken

Pee Wee spent every spare moment near the stallion, letting it get his smell. It refused to eat from his hand and after the initial walk home, it reversed behavior by rearing and pawing the ground whenever anyone came around.

Pee Wee thought of his father, Two Bears, and how he broke the wild ones. He spent time around them and refused to go back in the tepee. Morning Dove placed his food away from the camp so Two Bears would not change his scent. Pee Wee didn't have that luxury. He had to do chores, which brought smells to his clothing. He found the change in the stallion was due to the other animal smells. The stallion especially disliked the hog's odor and made Pee Wee run and dive under the fence every time he entered the corral.

When he was alone, Pee Wee solved most of the problem, by wearing a breech cloth. He rubbed dust on his body to kill the odors of the farm animals.

"I will sleep near his corral, so he will get to know me."

James shook his head. "You'll sleep in the house like always, where I can keep an eye on you." He locked the door from the inside at night, but Pee Wee had never given up on escaping. He would need a few more years in order to survive on the trail. He was tall and wiry now as he neared his twelfth summer and the chores had given him strength.

* * *

James put Pee Wee in the corral daily and laughed heartily as the stallion drove him away. "I thought you was a bronc fighter, Pee Wee. Bronc fighters don't run and dive under the fence. Get in there and break him."

Pee Wee never answered the taunts. He was not afraid of the stallion and tried to get close to him each time he was in the corral. The stallion accepted him more when wearing the breechcloth. As the weeks grew into months, Pee Wee slowly won over the stallion. He could pet him and brush him and one day he slipped upon its back. All friendship vanished as the stallion felt the weight and turned wild. Pee Wee didn't last but a few seconds before he was spinning in the sky. He got back on only to be thrown again and again. After several weeks, Pee Wee was able to last the bucking, crow hopping and sun fishing almost to the end.

* * *

The next time he was put in the corral, Pee Wee was wearing the breechcloth to James's dismay. "What are you wearing? You trying to mock me or something, Boy? Get that thing off right now and put some clothes on." James turned towards the house. "Cecelia sees you in that thing and you'll regret it."

"The Stallion does not like the smells of the other animals. I wear these only to get rid of the smells. I can ride him if I wear this."

"I don't believe you can ride him at all. That horse can't be ridden." James glanced towards the house. "I'll give you a chance and you better ride him 'cause if you don't, I'm going to bust your hide."

Pee Wee slipped under the fence and headed to the Stallion. He held out his hand offering a few oats. The Stallion hesitated then slowly came forward to eat the oats.

"What in the world!" James exclaimed. "How did you get him to do that?"

Pee Wee spoke softly and saddled the Stallion. He sprang into the saddle and prepared for the battle. He was not disappointed. The Stallion reared then put his head between his legs and shot Pee Wee into the air.

"Haw! Haw! Haw! I thought you said you could ride him?" James cried getting into the spirit of the action.

Pee Wee barely hit the saddle again till the stallion was twisting and twirling first right and then left. As Pee Wee hit the ground with a thud, James slapped his knee. "My Grandmother could ride better than that."

Pee Wee took a run and jumped into the saddle. The Stallion reared and put his head between his legs, but Pee Wee was set and leaned back almost lying down on the horse. As the Stallion's head came up, Pee Wee leaned forward.

"That's the way to ride 'em, Cowboy," James cried waving his hat in the air.

The Stallion fought, but he seemed to be just going through the motions and not trying hard to buck Pee Wee off. Finally, he snorted and shook his head as Pee Wee rode him around the corral.

James jumped the fence. "Danged if you didn't do it. I would never have thought you could fan him, but you did it! You did it!"

Pee Wee brought the Stallion to a halt.

"Get off my horse and let me try him out. I'll be the talk of the town now that people see that I broke him."

James mounted the Stallion and fought the little defense that he put up, but Pee Wee had tamed him. "Yes siree! I can put him with the mares now. I'm going to have the best herd around. Wait till Bob sees me riding this black. Man, oh man will he be upset that he traded him away."

Pee Wee sat on the top rail and felt miserable that the Stallion was broken. He preferred him to be wild and free. James trotted past Pee Wee. "Get your clothes on before Cecelia sees you."

Pee Wee headed to the barn without a backward glance. He didn't care, when he noticed Cecelia had heard the commotion and was watching.

CHAPTER NINE

Death

James was the envy of everyone in town as he pranced past on the Stallion. He told everyone how he had fought the Stallion to a stand-still. "Old Pee Wee couldn't fan him. He's just a boy. I had to show him how it's done. I climbed on him and he knew he had met his Master. Liked to have snapped me into, but I beat him down. He's just like a puppy dog, now. Even little kids could ride him, but I wouldn't want to chance it. He's still wild, you know."

Men clapped James on the back and congratulated him over and over. He strutted around glad-handing and smiling. Pee Wee didn't care that he didn't get the credit. He knew how White Eyes had forked tongues.

Bob offered James six top mares for the Black, but James refused to trade. "He's going to build my herd. Going to be the best ones around."

Hatred burned in Bob's eyes. He should've let Pee Wee break the horse while he still owned it, but he hated Indians too much, especially Pee Wee.

"He's just too good at Cowboying,' he muttered. "It ain't right for an Indian to beat White Boys at the rodeo."

* * *

Pee Wee was in luck after the raid. He found a bow and quiver of arrows, that James hadn't destroyed and hid them. When he was given a chore, he would hurry and finish, while James was busy elsewhere, then spend a few minutes practicing with the bow and arrows. He shot into hay so as not to lose or damage the arrows.

At first, the bow was much too large for him, so he held it sideways to shoot. He couldn't draw the bow far enough to employ the tactics that Standing Elk had taught him to use to shoot straight, but he enjoyed just having the bow. As the months went by, Pee Wee could now hold the bow upright, draw it all the way and shoot straight.

* * *

It wasn't long before the Enemy came in search of the black stallion, for the news had traveled fast. But James kept him staked close to the house. Pee Wee still slept on the floor and watched the horizon in the dark, dreaming of his freedom. He saw the movement at the corral and knocked on the bedroom door.

"The Enemy is here!" James came running out of the house, shooting the buffalo gun. Pee Wee ran to the barn and retrieved his bow and arrows. He was going to shoot a raider, when the moon came from behind a cloud and he recognized Running Horse.

Pee Wee crept close and whispered, "Brother. It is Gray Fox. Why do you raid the White Eyes?"

"We have joined the Enemy's band. Our band is too small to live on its own."

"Our tribe lives! I would like to join you and leave this place. I cannot live like a dog any longer."

"The big White Eyes is dead. Come with us and be free."

"I cannot now. I must go back. I must wait or I will be blamed for killing him."

Running Horse nodded. "There is a stand of trees by the stream that flows to the big water. I will meet you there in two moons."

Pee Wee hid his bow and arrows and looked for James' body. He went to the cabin and knocked on the bedroom door. "The Enemy has killed James," he said in perfect English.

Cecelia screamed and went running out to the porch. "You murdering Savage. You did this. I saw you with the bow and arrows and riding around naked, but James wouldn't listen."

"I did not kill him. It was the Enemy. See, their bodies are still on the ground. Why would I wait seven years to kill him, when I could have killed him at any time? I thought my mother and father dead and my tribe gone. Why would I kill him, when I had no place to go?"

"Well, you can't stay here. I never wanted you in the first place. Murdering Heathen. Desecrating my boy's clothes. You can help me bury him and then you can get out. I never want to see your Heathen face again."

"If I am to leave, then I will go now. You can dig the grave or tie a rope to his leg and drag him into the woods for the animals like he does the others. I am no longer Pee Wee! I am Gray Fox! I will take one horse for my seven years of labor. I chose the black stallion."

"That's right, you murdering Devil. Take the best horse we got. I'll have the Vigilantes on you and they'll fix your wagon."

"I have murdered no one and you know it. My seven years of labor are worth the horse. I was brought here against my will and forced to stay. I was beaten till I learned your language and your ways. I was treated like a dog, but did the work of a man. If I were a murdering Savage, I would kill you where you stand, burn this place to the ground and take all your horses."

Gray Fox spun on his heels and went to the barn. He retrieved the bow and arrows, mounted the black stallion and rode out. "Let them come," he said, "Now that we are part of a larger tribe, we will be able to fight the White Eyes."

***

Within a short distance he caught the Raiders and joined their band. "It is good to see you Running Horse. I thought you dead."

"Aiiieee!" Running Horse exclaimed. "You have the great black one. It is good!"

"Who do you live with? Is there room for me in your tepee?"

"Yes. I live with your Mother and Father. I was just made a Warrior. This is my first raid. I brought them here for the Black, but I was hoping to find you and take you home."

"They are still alive? I saw my Father shot and my Mother beaten down when she tried to save me."

"Your Mother was only bruised. She had trouble walking and seeing for many moons, but she is good now. Your Father has healed from his wound, but he cannot use his arm. It hangs like a dead, withered branch in winter. His spirit is weak, that is why he did not come to save you."

Sorrow struck Gray Fox's heart, but he was glad they were still alive. "So, we are now part of the Enemy?"

"No, we are still a small band living on the corner of their land. I joined them, so I could rescue you. After you were captured, I tracked the White Eyes to see where they had taken you. I stole this horse and used it to pull your father to safety on a travois in case they came back.

The White Eyes have raided the Enemy many times since you left, but the Enemy is too strong for the White Eyes. We have killed many White Eyes. Tonight, I laid in wait and killed their Chief. I have watched his ways many times, while holding the horses. I knew which way he would come and where he would make his stand. I was waiting for him and sank my arrow deep. He was the one who led them on the raids. Now that he is dead, they will come no more."

"No, he was just one leader of one band. There are many bands and they will come to avenge his death. She will tell them I stole this horse and killed him for she saw me practicing with this bow and arrow. I took the horse for payment of my work. I could have taken them all, but I did not. I only took one, not wanting to leave her poor."

* * *

They rode for a few moons till they came to the camp. The size of the village surprised Gray Fox. He was used to seeing a small band of Indians. He felt like weeping when he saw what was left of his tribe.

"Gray Fox! Gray Fox!" His mother ran to meet him for Running Horse had told her of his plans. "It is not good that you have joined the Enemy," she had said, "but I know it must be to rescue Gray Fox."

* * *

Two Bears was just a figure of his former self. He was thin and withdrawn. He sat and stared most of the time. He seemed to barely notice his son was home.

As they sat around the fire that night, Running Horse said, "You must tell us of your time with the White Eyes."

"It is not good to hear. They call us Savages, Heathens and Murderers, but they are worse than we are. They kill for pleasure, not to defend their land or for revenge against an enemy. They kill for joy and they kill each other over little things like words or thoughts. They talk with a forked tongue and have no pride in themselves or for any others. Their greed runs wild as the deer in the forest when chased by Brother Wolf. It would be better if we all moved to the Father of Waters, that White Feather talked about many moons ago. We could have many summers of peace before they arrive. There are so many White Eyes we cannot stop them. They swarm like the ants that have found food."

Running Horse waved his hand. "But we are many now. They cannot defeat us."

"You have not seen their towns and villages. They are not just one tribe. They are many tribes banded together. They cannot understand each other's talk and do not like each other, but they all hate us. They want our land and will kill us to get it. You cannot believe their paper or their talk. Lies rest on their tongues like a frog's waiting for a fly. They shoot out at any moment.

One group will sign a paper, and another will come and say the paper does not mean anything to them. The same goes when they give their word. They will give you the hand of friendship with one hand and stick you with a knife in the back with the other. They treat each other this way and will treat us no different."

"Aiiiieee!" Running Horse said. "What kind of people are they?"

"They are not of the Great Spirit, but of the evil one. They claim to know and love the Great Spirit but speak with forked tongues. Even the ones that say they are His servants will treat you the same as the others do. They only want to change us, so we can serve them. They have a saying: "the only good Indian (which is what they call us) is a dead Indian. No matter what they say, they all believe this."

"Then there is no hope for peace?" Morning Dove asked.

"No Mother. Only when we are their servants or dead, will they be satisfied," Gray Fox replied.

CHAPTER TEN

The Raid

The crickets chirped and the firelight reflected off Two Bears as Gray Fox talked with his father. Two Bears stared at the dark distant hills and didn't seem to be listening.

"Don't you want revenge for what they have done to you?" Gray Fox asked.

"They are too strong and have Thundersticks. We cannot defeat them." Two Bears replied.

"Maybe so, but we can kill some, take their horses and win many honors," Gray Fox said.

"We will all die," Two Bears said. "It is better to leave the White Eyes alone."

"It is a good way to die," Gray Fox said. "Didn't you say it was better to die in battle than in sleep?"

Two Bears paused for a few seconds as if in thought. "I was wrong. It is useless to fight the White Eyes. If we leave them alone, they will leave us alone."

"No so, my father. I have heard them speak many times. They forgot that I could understand their language.

They want us dead so they can take our land. If we fight or if we do nothing, they will take our land. So, it is better to die in battle. Won't you lead us, Father?"

Two Bears shook his head. "I can no longer handle the bow. It would have been better if I had died from my wounds."

"Father, you were a brave warrior. You still have wisdom and could lead raids and cause the White Eyes much harm. We would have more time."

"I would only be in the way." Two Bears closed his eyes and soon began to snore.

Gray Fox gazed at his father. He remembered how strong and proud he was and now he was content to sit in the sun with the old ones. He looked at the withered arm and wondered how he would feel if his arm were that way. Maybe it is better for him to be safe. Gray Fox went looking for Running Horse. "I would like to go with you on raids and hold the horses. I am not one to sit in the sun."

Running Horse glanced towards Two Bears. "He suffered much while waiting for his arm to heal. The wound did much damage. Your Mother's medicine could not help. When the arm withered, so did his spirit"

"I do not blame him, but someone must fight the White Eyes. They want our lands and to put us on a Reservation."

"What is that?" Running Horse asked.

"It means that we must leave here and stay in a certain place forever. We can no longer roam free to hunt the buffalo or deer."

"But this is our home. Living in one place will use up the grass in a few moons from our horses."

"We will no longer need horses, bow or arrows. The White Eyes will give us food."

"But how will we buy a wife or trade if we have no horses?"

"We must change our ways and accept the White Eyes ways?"

"Why are his ways better than our ways?"

"Because he is stronger." Gray Fox said.

Anger flashed in Running Horse's eyes. "Then we will fight to keep the ways of our fathers."

* * *

Gray Fox held the horses as Running Horse with a few others crept toward the corral. He glanced at the waning moon lighting up the area as if it were day. Surveying the terrain, he brought his eyes back to the band that had reached the corral. A pang of guilt hit his heart for he knew the White Eyes that lived here. He had sat on the top rail of that corral many times while James visited. It was true that they never accepted him and acted as if he weren't there, but over the years he had come to know them.

His heart leaped when he saw the door of the cabin open and Sam Hoskins step out. The neighing of a horse had alerted him. His Thunderstick roared once before and arrow found his heart. Running Horse gave his battle cry as he drove the horses ahead of him. Gary Fox caught up to him as they paused on the other side of the stream.

"I thought he had killed you," Gary Fox's eyes scanned Running Horse for wounds.

Running Horse was jubilant. "I only leaned down when I saw the light appear. My Spirit Guide is strong. I was not worried."

"You have many good horses. The best ones are at the Jergens' ranch, but he has many men working for him. It would be very dangerous to try and take his horses."

"The more danger the more honor. You will guide us to this place, and we will see how good his horses are."

Gray Fox pointed to the moon. "It is far. Brother Moon is going to sleep. We will have to go another time."

Running Horse laughed. "I do not want to wait long. Someone else may take his horses."

CHAPTER ELEVEN

Jergens

A week later, Brother Moon was full, but the night was eerie silent as the little band lay on the knoll and surveyed the Jergens' ranch. No night birds called, nor did any night animals venture forth. It was if they knew about the raid. Gray Fox had dreaded coming for he knew how many men were in the bunkhouse. It would be very dangerous to try and steal the good horses for they were rounded up each night and kept in the corral.

"Two Dogs will lead a few braves to collect the horses in the far pasture," Running Horse said.

"Be careful," Gray Fox said. "Men sleep near-by in case of a raid."

"We will take care of the men," Two Dogs said with a grin and shook his bow. He led the small group away as the others bent low and peered over the crest of the knoll.

"I will have to go first," Gray Fox said. "He has laid a trap and I know how to spring it."

Running Horse grinned. "Your time with the White Eyes was not wasted. You have learned how to defeat them."

Gray Fox's smiled at the praise, but his heart raced as he hunched down and led the group forward. He paused several times to make sure nothing had changed and had them rub dust on their bodies to hide their smell. He had learned from the Stallion that sometimes the horses did not like certain smells.

Jergens had strung empty airtight containers on a string across the gate. The cans would rattle when an unsuspecting hand tried to open the gate. Gray Fox carefully removed the string of cans and placed them to the side.

He opened the gate and slipped inside. He was just mounting a near-by horse when gunfire erupted from the direction Two Dogs had gone. Stampeding the horses, Grays Fox lay on the horse's' back to present a smaller target, when the door to the bunkhouse flew open and the men poured out firing their guns.

"It's that murdering kid, Pee Wee," Jergens shouted running towards the corral. "He's the only one that knew about the trap. Shoot him down."

Gray Fox herded the horses out of the corral. As he came out the gate, he was jerked from the horse by Jergens' strong hand.

"We got you now, you murdering Redskin, and we're going to make you pay." Jergens shouted. "Get a rope, Boys."

Gray Fox fought to get loose. "I have killed no one," he said in perfect English. "James was killed in battle, but not by me. I warned him the Enemy was trying to steal his horses."

"You're a liar," Jergens cried. "Cecelia told us how you sneaked in and murdered him in his bed."

"If that were true, why didn't I kill her? She never liked me nor accepted me. She treated me like a dog and made me eat on the porch. If I were to kill anyone, it would have been her."

Jergens cracked Gray Fox across the face so hard, he was jerked out of his hand. "You're a murdering dog. Killing the hand that feeds you after James took you in and tried to civilize you."

Gray Fox stared at Jergens. "Like the White Eyes are civilized? You take the land that is not yours and kill women and children. When we retaliate you say we are Savages. We want peace, but you want war."

"Come on with that rope," Jergens called and snatched Gray Fox from the ground.

Gray Fox was hastily put on a horse and a rope thrown over the barn rafter that was used to hoist hay to the loft. "Now, you'll pay for your crimes," Jergens cried fixing the rope around Gray Fox's neck.

"You say we are Heathens, but you are the ones that speak with a forked tongue. You know James did not break the Stallion. I did! You lost your best horse and that is why you want to hang me. You can't have an Indian better than a White Man. And it is also why you gave all my trophies to the second-place winners in the rodeo."

"This will shut your blabbering mouth, you murdering Red-devil," Jergens' slapped the horse and Gray Fox was jerked from its back to swing in the evening breeze.

The sky was filled with flaming arrows that set the barn ablaze. One struck the rope around Gray Fox's neck and he fell to the ground. War cries sounded and the little band came herding the horses into the Cowhands, scattering them and knocking the men down. Running Horse buried his Tomahawk in Jergens' skull. He gave Gray Fox a hand and pulled him up behind him on the horse. It happened so fast that only White Eyes were killed. Standing Elk and Black Hawk were wounded as the band herded the horses away.

Bullets whizzed by their head as they gained distance. Gray Fox tried to join Running Horse in the war cry as the horses thundered over the knoll, but his throat hurt too badly. The thrill of excitement flowed through his veins as they paused and Gray Fox mounted the Black Stallion. The raid had been successful and against overwhelming odds. He would get his pick of the fine mares for leading the raid and could build a great herd with the Stallion. He already knew which ones he wanted. The Bay mare, the White faced one and the Brown with the black tail. The White mare, the Red and Blue roans. These were the top mares in the Jergens herd. Gray Fox had coveted them on the many times he had visited the ranch.

"Here are the others," Running Horse shouted as he pointed towards the horses Two Dogs was bringing.

As they slowed the pace, all were jubilant at their success. "You did well," Two Dogs said envying the mares.

"We did not get the ones they ride," Gray Fox said. "The sound of the Thundersticks brought the men out."

The smile left Two Dogs face. "Little Elk and Red Arrow were not successful in killing all the guards. They will not be joining us in the victory dance."

Gray Fox's heart sank. "Two more young braves dead. Soon there would be no more braves to defend the tribe.

"We must find a place to hide," Gray Fox said. "They will follow us many moons to get these horses back, even though Jergens and several of his men are dead."

"I know a place where we can hide and help the wounded," Running Horse cried and led them back to the tribe's old camping site. Follow the stream behind the water-fall," he said.

The little band herded the horses through the falls and into a small green valley. Gray Fox was amazed as he surveyed the land. "I never knew this was here," he said.

"It was a secret," Running Horse said. "This is where the women, children and old ones came when there was a raid. It was how our tribe survived. You were young so probably do not remember."

Gray Fox nodded. "This is the place of my dreams. I did not know it was here. I thought we would find it when we followed Father Sun to his sleeping place."

"We can stay here for a while, till they give up trying to find us," Running Horse said.

"That will be several moons," Gary Fox replied. "They may get discouraged soon now that Jergens is dead and they have no one to lead them. I hope our grass holds out."

"We can send Two Dogs to see when they return to their place," Running Dog explained."

"It is a good plan," Gray Fox said.

CHAPTER TWELVE
Thundersticks

As the small group of Warriors from his tribe gathered around him, Gray Fox held up the rifle he had taken on a raid. "This Thunderstick is called a rifle. It is not to be feared. You will get used to the noise. I have never fired one, but I have seen it done many times. I know how to load them and to make bullets for them. It is important that we learn how to use them if we are to survive."

The small group cheered. He went through the procedures for loading the rifle. Next he showed them how to hold it and aim. When the rifle fired, he couldn't belief the recoil against his shoulder. Then he remembered that James always held his rifle tight against his shoulder. Each Warrior took a turn at firing the rifle.

When the Enemy heard the rifle fire, they came running. "What is this that you do?" Big Turtle cried. "We thought it a raid."

"We are learning how to use the White Eyes Thundersticks so we can defeat them," Running Horse replied.

"You learn so you can defeat us," Big Turtle said.

"It is not true," Gray Fox said. "We will only use them against the White Eyes. You have been kind to us. We will not use them against you."

"If this is true, why do you not show us?" Standing Horse asked. "We are many and need stronger weapons."

"We only have one," Running Horse said. "Since we are only a few, we thought to learn first and then to show you after we have taken more."

"Show us now!" Standing Horse demanded. "We will learn together!"

"Collect rifles on your raids," Gray Fox said. "Also, collect the bullets that goes with each one for some rifles are not the same."

After the others had left, they sat around the fire, Running Horse smiled. "It is good to know about the rifle. Now, we can defeat the White Eyes."

Gray Fox shook his head. "No. We can not defeat them, but we can slow their progress. With the Enemy needing rifles it will take much time to collect rifles and to practice to kill. We will need many rifles and bullets. I know where they are stored."

"Then we will go to this place and take them," Running Horse said.

"It will be very dangerous for it is in their village. It is the place where they trade. There are many White Eyes in the village with many rifles. If the White Eyes find us, we may not survive."

Running Horse laughed. "Then we will be as quiet as the deer in the forest. If not, it is a good day to die."

Gray Fox nodded. "The White Eyes sleep like Brother Bear in the cold, but like Brother Bear, he is fierce if awakened."

* * *

The next night the moon slid behind a cloud as Gray Fox harnessed Stillman's horses and wagon. He again had covered his smell with dust, so the horses wouldn't reject him. He placed the wagon near the front door.

"He sleeps in the rear, so we must be careful," Gray Fox whispered. He used his knife to lift the bolt and open the door. The little band slipped into the store and loaded the rifles. Gray Fox handed boxes of ammunition to them. Just as they were about to leave, Black Hawk dropped his box of ammunition.

"Who's there?" Stillman called. "Who's out there?"

Gray Fox motioned the others to leave. They had almost made it out the door when Stillman came through the curtains.

"Pee Wee!" He exclaimed. "You murdering Savage."

Gray Fox's throw sank his knife deep into Stillman's chest. His pistol discharged several times into the floor as he fell. Gray Fox ran out the door and sprang onto the wagon seat. He had driven wagons many times and led the band out of town at a gallop. Doors were opened and lantern's held high as men exited their homes.

"It's an Indian attack," Newt yelled firing his rifle at the fleeing group. Running Antelope, Gray Bird and Little Crow of the Enemy band fell as bullets flew after the band making its way out of town.

"They robbed Stillman's," Newt yelled running into the store. "They've killed him. That's Pee Wee's knife! I'd know it anywhere! Let's get him boys! He's leading his band to kill all the White Folks that befriended him."

By the time the men saddled their horses and began the chase, the little Indian band had made it to James' place. Gray Fox had found out that Cecelia had sold the ranch and gone back east. They had killed the new owners, burned the ranch and brought back the horses. Gray Fox was sure Running Horse had planned the raid for revenge, when he had told him of his life there.

The destruction of the ranch did not erase the dreadful memories as Gray Fox backed the wagon into the standing hay. There were many wagon tracks on the dusty road and so they were not easily tracked.

"They will not look for us here," Gray Fox said. "There are no buildings for us to hide in."

"Your life was cruel," Running Horse said, "but you have learned enough about the White Eyes that they cannot defeat us."

Gray Fox shook his head. "Even with guns we will not defeat them. There are many. There are lands across large waters where many White Eyes live. They are as the fires in the sky with Brother Moon." Gray Fox pointed to the starry sky. "The more we kill the more will come for our lands. They have large guns that speak loud as thunder and will kill many braves and horses at one time."

"You have seen these guns shoot?" Running Horse asked.

"No, but I have seen them in drawings and heard James tell of them. They are called cannons and their bullets are bigger than our heads."

Running Horse laughed till he fell over. "These are stories to tell around the campfire," he said once he had gained control.

"No, James did not laugh when he spoke of them. They are pulled by several horses and take several men to shoot them. I have seen them in their writings called History books. They speak truth."

"Bah!" Running Horse dismissed the conversation with a wave of his hand. "I will not believe till I see."

"Ask the Great Spirit that you never see them."

Running Horse shook his head. "These are things to scare little papooses."

"No," Gray Fox said. "The White Eyes have fought many wars with each other. We did not believe Thundersticks were so. Now we carry them. These weapons are also true. When they come we will be easily defeated."

"Then let us kill the White Eyes till they bring them," Running Horse cried.

* * *

For several years they had success against the White Eyes. Gray Fox had heard James and others discuss battles and had learned their tactics. They seemed to forget that he had been forced to learn their language and talked as if he were not there.

"After the raid, placing our warriors on each side of the trail will put the White Eyes in a crossfire," Gray Fox crossed his wrists.

"Won't they see our warriors and kill them?" Running Horse asked.

"We will use rocks, trees and ravines to hide. We will dig shallow holes, like the White Eyes do for their dead. We will cover our men with blankets and put a layer of dirt over them. When the White Eyes ride past, they will rise up and attack from behind."

Running Horse laughed at the prospect of ambushing the White Eyes.

"We will drop from trees and rocks to kill the last one in line. We will take the horse and be gone before the others know what happened."

Running Horse grinned. "These are good plans. Soon the White Eyes will not be so quick to chase us."

CHAPTER THIRTEEN

Rescue

For several more years, Gray Fox moved happily around the camp and went on raids that were led by Running Horse. He enjoyed the freedom of this way of life and was glad he no longer had to do chores. Gray Fox taught others how to load and fire rifles and to shoot from a running horse. He did not think his teaching them how to shoot and clean their guns was important and was glad when he finally became a Warrior and could ride at the front to kill the White Eyes invading his land.

He was no longer a little boy but had grown taller and filled out. His hair was long and made into plaits that hung down on each side of his face. He wore an Eagle feather in it to show he was a Warrior. He didn't wear the feather, but a cowboy hat, shirt, leggings and moccasins, when he slipped into town to hide behind the bushes and listen at the store window to the White Eyes.

* * *

"Where did you get these prime furs?" asked Bob Stillwater, the new owner of the General Store.

"Bear Mountain," the beaded trapper replied. "Me and Zeke spent the winter up there."

"Weren't you afraid of the Indians?" Bob asked. "They've been killing any white man found on their land."

"Zeke laughed. "Me and Lars ain't afraid of any Indian. We kilt plenty of them."

"If you're going back, you better be wary of Pee Wee." Bob replied checking the furs.

"Who'd that be?" Zeke asked.

"An Indian boy that was raised by James and Cecelia Griffin. Took him in 'cause he was an orphan. The ungrateful cuss turned around and murdered James in his bed to escape, then brought his murdering friends back, burned the ranch and run off with their prized horses. Then he came back and murdered Jergens after him being so kind to that Red Devil."

"Me and Lars know how to take care of him if he comes nosing around us."

"All the same I would be careful." Bob said taking the furs into the back room.

* * *

Two days later, Gray Fox listened to the mountain men talking as Brother Moon crept across the sky in the desolate mountains halfway to Bear Mountain. He was perched in a tree above them as they went about getting ready for sleep.

"Vhat do you tink about dat Pee Vee fella."

"He ain't going to fool with us, Lars. We're too cagey for him. He won't come to Bear Mountain. It's too fur away. Sides, ain't we got us a couple squaws we captured locked up to protect us. They won't fool with us as long as they're with us."

"I'd yust like to get him in my sites vone time." Lars said.

"You're the best shot I know of," Zeke said. "He'll sure be a dead Indian if he fools with us."

***

Gray Fox waited till they had been asleep awhile before he slipped from the tree. He took their moccasins, guns, knives, supplies and horses. As he rode away, he left a little trail of food. Putting the horses safely above the cave, he threw pebbles in till he heard the angry bear growling. He was well above the entrance when the grizzly came barreling out. Gray Fox nodded when the bear began following the food trail.

Lars and Zeke bolted awake when they heard the roar. Lars surveyed the scene and saw the bear. "Vere's are our guns and knifs?"

Zeke eyes widened at the sight of the grizzly standing on his hind legs. "Make for the tree!" he shouted.

Scrambling as high as they could get, they felt safe till the tree began to weave back and forth.

"Vat happened to our supplies?"

"Never mind about them. Look out, Lars! He's pushing the tree over."

The men's screams could be heard for miles as the tree crashed to earth.

"Make for the river, Lars." Zeke took off running down the hill. The bear sniffed Lars' dead body then took off in hot pursuit of Zeke.

Cuts and bruises on his tender feet were ignored as Zeke raced ahead. Nearing the river, a stumped and bleeding toe ended his run as he plunged head-first from the mountain into the flowing stream.

..*

Gray Fox arrived at the men's camp and surveyed the area. The cabins sat side by side in a glen. The windows were made of boards that were raised upward to let in the light and to cool the cabins. The windows were blocked on the outside so they couldn't be raised. The door on one cabin was also blocked. Gray Fox headed to the blocked door and called softly. "I am Gray Fox. I have come to set you free. Do not kill me when I open the door."

Two pretty young girls came out carrying their children. They were both of the Enemy's tribe. The girls looked to be about fifteen or sixteen.

The taller one said, "I am called Morning Sun and my little one is called, Aaron. The boy looked to be about a year old.

"I am called Blue Flower and my little one is called, Faith. Her baby looked to be about six months old.

"Why is it you have our husband's horses?" Morning Sun asked.

Gray Fox smiled. "I captured them while they slept. I will take you away."

"We cannot go. They always follow us and beat us." Blue Flower glanced towards the trial.

"I do not think they will come back. Brother Bear came to see them."

"Then we will go with you. But you must promise to protect us," Morning Sun said.

"I promise. How is it you are here?"

"We were gathering berries when we were taken from behind. We were tied and beaten when we tried to escape. We were locked in when they went to the traps."

The girls gathered their belongings while Gray Fox destroyed the corral. He set the cabins ablaze as they headed down the trail. "We need to spring the traps," Gray Fox said.

"They did not set them while they were gone," Blue Flower replied.

Gray Fox didn't have to protect them. They discovered Lars body on the way back and Gray Fox later heard of the finding of Zeke's body twenty miles downstream. The pretty girls soon found husbands.

CHAPTER FOURTEEN

Newt

Newt kept a wary eye on his surroundings as he headed towards town. The news of Pee Wee's raids struck fear into his heart. The brazen attacks and the ambushes afterward left the strongest man quivering in his bed. Even the men in town walked in fear of an attack at any moment, even though the settlement was now twice as big. Regardless of the threat of an attack, settlers were pouring into town, waiting for the Indian trouble to be settled, so they could claim a farm, build a cabin and sow their crops.

"Why I've killed many Indians," Newt bragged to anyone who would listen. "I have led many raids and even had a hand to hand fight with Two Bears, one of the fiercest Warriors that ever walked the earth."

"Gosh!" would emit from the mouths of his audience, which were composed of children.

"Why, we rolled around, kicking up dust, gouging and biting till I sunk my knife into his shoulder. Left him a cripple to this day. Now, he just sits in the sun with the old men. Not an ounce of fight left in him."

"Why didn't you kill him?" someone would ask.

"I would have, except the tribe showed up and I had to hightail it."

* * *

Fall was just making an appearance, when Newt paused his horse as the birds quieted and stillness prevailed in the afternoon sun. He checked the area, but all seemed natural. The flowers were wilting from lack of rain and the rootless tumbleweeds lay idle. He glanced towards the sky and saw a hawk flap his wings and disappear. Newt swallowed several times even though his mouth had gone dry. He nudged his horse. "Come on, Hector. It's too far to go back to the ranch. Best to just keep going to town."

"Hello Newt!"

"Gasp!" Newt's heart leaped in his chest as he turned to see Gray Fox. He barely recognized the youth sitting the black Stallion beside him. The paint on the face and body made the once handsome boy into a scary monster. The long lithe body rippled with muscles and he sat the Black with ease. "Where'd you come from?"

"Being such a great Woodsman, Newt, I'm surprised you didn't see me. I was right behind you for the last few miles."

Newt's Adam's apple danced as he looked back at the vacant prairie. "You couldn't have…" Newt must have thought better of finishing the sentence when he saw the countenance change beneath the paint. "I-I-I'm not calling you a lair. I guess my eyes ain't what they used to be."

A smile played at the young man's lips. Just a few short years ago, Newt thought nothing of spanking and cuffing him around and now he sat in terror of the Warrior that faced him.

Gray Fox placed the butt of the rifle against his thigh. "How have you been, Newt?"

"Just fine." Newt appeared to let out the breath that he had been holding. "We're friends, ain't we Pee Wee?"

The smile quickly vanished, and a stern look replaced it at the mention of the hated name. "Friends! Let's see. If I remember correctly, it was your idea to put me on the calves for everyone's enjoyment. And it was your idea to have me rope calves that were bigger than me and you laughed the hardest when they drug me through cactus. And it was your idea to put me on this Stallion hoping he would kill me."

Fear crept into Newt's eyes as each item was mentioned. "I meant no harm. Putting you on the calves is how you became a good bronc rider. I was really helping you."

The large vein in Newt's neck throbbed faster and faster as the silence grew. Gray Fox words broke the quiet. "You say we are friends? When I was wrestling Bucky and Wally and winning, wasn't it you, that pulled me off and said I was using dirty Indian tricks?"

"Gulp!" Newt's eyes widened as anger flashed in Gray Fox's eyes.

"And didn't you say, I needed a whipping and when James said he would whip me at home, wasn't it you that yelled: 'Don't wait. It's never too late to learn him how to behave with decent folks?' And after James kicked me, didn't you shout: 'Kick him again. Once more won't hurt him and might teach him a lesson?'

Sweat streaked Newt's face as fear reeked from his body. His eyes seemed riveted to Gray Fox's face

"Tell me again how you fought my father and crippled him till there wasn't an ounce of fight left in him. And how he now sits in the sun with old men."

"How did you know about me saying that?"

"Why Newt. You're so famous your words even get around to us Savages. Tell me how I murdered James in his bed and then came back with my bloodthirsty band and killed poor Cecelia and burnt the ranch. You know those kind White Folks that took in an ungrateful Orphan and tried to teach him Christian values, but he was too stupid to learn."

"It was just talk, Pee Wee. You know how an old man gets things mixed up. Everyone knows Cecelia sold the ranch and moved back east."

"I seem to recall that you were at the back of the pack that raided a defenseless village for a raid you knew we didn't commit. How brave James shot my father with a 50-caliber buffalo gun, then clubbed my mother in the head with the stock and kidnapped me. Not to mention, you weren't even at the ranch when James was killed to know how he really died, or you wouldn't be here."

Tears streamed down Newt's beard. "I'm sorry, Pee Wee." It was just an old man's talk. I was trying to be somebody. You know."

The silence grew as tears flooded Newt's face and the vein throbbed. The steady gaze seemed to be recalling every word and deed Newt had said or did. When Gray Fox shifted on his horse, it startled Newt. He grabbed his chest and fell. Gray Fox looked down at the gaping mouth and staring eyes. He took Newt's reins, nudged his horse and rode on.

CHAPTER FIFTEEN
A New Chief

The fall evening breeze made the smoke change as Gray Fox and Running Horse sat around the fire. "I think we should move to the Father of Waters," Gray Fox announced as he shifted away from the smoke. The White Eyes grow stronger and move closer every day."

"But we are strong!" Running Horse exclaimed. "Now that we have guns, they cannot defeat us. We should remain here and gain much honor."

"Yes, with the Enemy we are strong, but the White Eyes are stronger. Our little band should leave while we still have people left. I crept into their town and heard them talk of building forts for large bands of soldiers and bringing the cannons I told you about. We are so far away from the Enemy camp we could easily be defeated. One or two shots from the cannons would kill all our people.

Also, I do not like the looks that the Enemy give us when we take our share after a raid. I think they would like to rid us from their land. We may soon find ourselves fighting two Enemies instead of just the White

Eyes. I have to watch the Stallion all the time to keep him from being stolen."

Running Horse nodded. "Who would lead us on our journey?"

"You are the only one that has become a strong Warrior and have won many honors in battle. You have a wife and children and the others respect and follow you. You will be our Chief."

Running Horse shook his head. "You also have a squaw. You be Chief. I am not good at leading people. A battle is a small thing and is over in a short time but making decisions for the people takes wisdom."

"We will help and advise you. I am too young. You are the only one the people will follow."

"Let us call a Council and let the people decide."

"See, that is your first wise decision." Gray Fox grinned and slapped Running Horse gently on the back. "You're IT, as the white children say in their game."

The tribe elected Running Horse Chief and he and Gray Fox went to Lame Bear, the new Enemy Chief, to let them know they were leaving.

"Give us half of your horses as payment for using our land," Lame Bear said.

"We can not. You never gave us protection, food or shelter. We have paid by helping to supply food, protection against the White Eyes and going on raids. I, myself, have led many raids with many horses for your people. We earned our stay."

"This is true," Lame Bear said. "We will miss you for you are a brave Warrior. Give us the big Stallion to build our herd and we will let you go."

"The Stallion is not mine to give. It belongs to Gray Fox," Running Horse nodded to Gray Fox.

"I need to watch all the time, so no one sneaks in and takes the Stallion, but I have put him with the herd many times, so it is stronger."

Lame Bear ignored the words that his Warriors would steal the Stallion. "It is true. The White Eyes want the Stallion back. They say Gray Fox killed the White Eye's Chief in sleep and stole the Stallion."

"They speak with forked tongue," Gray Fox said. "I was captured when I had only seen five summers. I spent seven more summers being beaten to learn the White Eye's way and their tongue. I earned much honor taming wild horses as my father, Two Bears, had done. When I was told to leave, I took only the Stallion as payment. I could have taken all the horses, but I did not."

"It is right that you took the Stallion. If I escaped, I would have taken the best horse." Lame Bear looked into the fire. "If Gray Fox did not kill the White Eyes Chief, who did?"

"I killed the White Eye's Chief in battle." Running Horse nodded towards the others. "Big Turtle was there. So was White Cloud and Black Dog."

They murmured agreement.

"The White Eyes was using his rifle. He died like a Warrior, not in his bed, as the White Eyes say. He was my first kill as a Warrior. They take away my honor with their forked tongues."

Lame Bear nodded.

Running Horse placed his hand on Gray Fox's shoulder. "Gray Fox has showed you how to use rifles. He has made you stronger against the White Eyes.

Lame Bear nodded. "This is true. For one so young he has done much to help defeat the While Eyes. He may keep his horse."

Gray Fox looked at Running Horse and he nodded. "I have gone into the White Eyes village when Brother Moon was sleeping and heard them speak of building forts." He drew one in the dust with his finger, "They will bring many soldiers with large guns to kill all." He drew a cannon and cannonball in the dust. When these are fired, they are like thunder and fire from the sky hitting a tree. One bullet kills many Braves and horses."

Running Horse spoke. "Since we are so far from your camp, we can be easily killed. We want to go to where Brother Sun sleeps, away from the White Eyes."

Lame Bear sat looking at the pictures in the dust. Furrowing his brow, he seemed to make a decision. "You may leave and move across our land."

"We thank you for letting us live here," Running Horse said. I give you these three horses and this rifle for your kindness."

"Go in peace. I have spoken." Lame Bear smiled as he accepted the horses and rifle.

..*

A few of the Enemy's young braves that had married into their tribe left with them, for they admired Running Horse for his courage and leadership. Also, they wanted to see new lands and the Father of Waters.

The End

Gray Fox was five years old when he was captured by the White Eyes and his name was changed to Pee Wee. He has mixed emotions about them as he matures. He hates them for taking him away from his parents, but after seven years he learns their ways. There are many stories about whites being captured and raised by the Indians, read on to see how it may have been in reverse.

About the author

Kenneth R Leonard, Sr. is a retired Elementary teacher and Guidance Counselor, who has been writing poetry, songs and short stories for most of his life. He is originally from the Appalachian Mountains in Pennsylvania, but now resides in Columbus, Ohio. Ken is the author of several novels to include Seth Bromley, Circuit Rider, Fool's Gold, Crime Stories, An Anthology, Sol Dorado, A Bullet for my Brother, Dabsy on Society, Missy, Skeeter, Whistle Pig in the Pines, Stagecoach West, Cowboy Campfire Poems, Christmas Memories in Stories and Poems,, Stories for the Young at Heart, and three books in The Bible in Poetry series and four in the Texas Slim, Ranger series. His books are available on Amazon and Kindle.